This book belongs to

. . . .

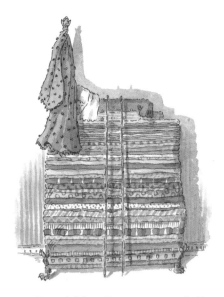

Retold by Ronne Randall
Illustrated by Anna C. Leplar

This is a Parragon Publishing Book
First published in 2005

Parragon Publishing
Queen Street House
4 Queen Street
Bath BA1 1HE, UK

Copyright © Parragon 2005

ISBN 1-40544-783-4

Printed in Indonesia

Hans Christian Andersen

The Princess
and the Pea

p

A long time ago, in a land far away, there lived a king and queen who had just one son. The prince was grown up, and it was time for him to marry a princess.

"And she must be a *real* princess," the prince told the king and queen.

But there were no princesses in the land where he lived, so the king and queen arranged for the prince to travel to strange and distant lands to find a bride.

The prince traveled north through frozen lands, until he came to a castle where a princess lived.

This princess was tall and fair, with skin as soft as a peach. But when she laughed she sounded like a braying donkey! And though she was smart, she was also vain and boastful.

"Not only am I exquisitely beautiful," she told the prince, "but I can name every capital city of every country in the world, and I can speak twenty-four languages! You will never meet anyone as smart as me!"

"A *real* princess would never be so boastful," thought the prince. "I can't marry her!"

So the prince traveled south through hot, sandy deserts, until he came to a palace where a princess lived.

This princess had long, gleaming hair the color of midnight, and skin that smelled of sweet almonds. She also had the most enormous feet!

But though she was very beautiful, the princess would not speak to the prince. She would not even smile at him. She held her pretty nose high in the air.

"A *real* princess would never be so proud," thought the prince. "I can't marry her!"

And so the disappointed prince traveled east through misty lands and over windswept mountains, until he came to a mansion where a princess lived.

This princess was small and neat, with rippling red hair. She had a charming smile and a lovely voice—but she told the most shocking lies!

"Last night I ate a whole elephant for dinner," she told the prince. "It was as big as this room!"

"Really?" said the prince. "How amazing!"

"A *real* princess would never tell such shocking lies," thought the prince. "I can't marry her!"

A year had passed when the prince returned home from his travels, weary, sad, and lonely.

"I will just have to remain a bachelor," he told the king and queen.

One evening, not long after the prince had come home, a terrible storm blew in from the west. Outside the window, lightning flashed and thunder rumbled, and huge raindrops fell from the sky.

Inside the palace, the prince sat with the king and queen by the fireside, listening to the storm.

Suddenly, there was a knock at the castle door! The king was so surprised that he went to answer it himself.

There, standing in the windy doorway, was the most bedraggled young woman the king had ever seen.

Water ran down her hair and face, and her clothes were sopping wet and muddy. Water ran in through the toes of her shoes and out again through the heels.

"Good evening, Your Majesty," she said to the king, curtsying politely. "I am a princess, and I need shelter for the night. May I please come in?"

The king could hardly believe that this soggy, sorry-looking creature was a princess, but he invited her in anyway.

"Of course," he said. "Please come in out of the storm. "We will gladly give you shelter for the night."

When the king told the prince that a princess had turned up at the door, the prince was very eager to meet her. But the queen told him he would have to wait.

"The princess said that she couldn't possibly meet you wet and bedraggled," the queen explained. "She has gone to have a bath and change into some dry clothes."

"That's a good sign," said the prince. "But how can we be certain that she is a *real* princess?"

"I have an idea," said his mother. "Just leave everything to me." Off went the queen to the kitchen. She asked the cook for a single, tiny, dried pea.

A short while later, the princess arrived in the main hall dressed in the queen's clothes. Her hair shone, her cheeks were rosy, and her eyes sparkled merrily to match her smile. She certainly looked like a real princess.

The prince and princess sat beside the fire and talked for hours. The princess was smart, charming and seemed honest. The prince was enchanted—but he still wasn't sure that the princess was a *real* princess.

Meanwhile, the queen went to the best guest bedroom carrying a single, tiny, dried pea.

In the bedroom, she put the pea under the bed mattress. Then she asked a servant to bring another mattress to put on top of the first, and then another mattress, and another, and another. At last there were TWENTY mattresses on the bed!

But even that wasn't enough. The queen told the servant to put twenty soft, cozy quilts on top of the twenty mattresses. Then she had a ladder brought for the princess.

As soon as the queen was satisfied that the bed was ready, she showed the sleepy princess to her room.

The princess was surprised when the queen brought her to the bedroom with its towering bed and tall ladder. But she didn't protest or complain. She thanked the queen and wished her good night.

The princess climbed the ladder to the very top of the pile of mattresses and quilts. Sighing contentedly, she settled down to sleep. But the princess did not sleep a wink. She tossed and turned all night.

By morning, the princess felt tired and weary. When she came down to breakfast, the prince, the king, and the queen greeted her eagerly.

"Did you sleep well?" asked the queen.

"I'm afraid not," sighed the princess. "There was something small and hard in the bed, and no matter which way I tossed and turned, I still felt it. I'm dreadfully tired, for I hardly slept at all."

"I'm so sorry," said the queen. "But I'm delighted, too! For this proves that you are indeed a *real* princess! Only a *real* princess would feel a tiny pea under twenty mattresses and twenty quilts!"

The prince was overjoyed, for he had already fallen in love with the princess—and she had fallen in love with him. And so they were married.

They had a splendid wedding, and they invited all the royal families of all the kingdoms the prince had visited.

And what happened to the pea? It was put on a velvet cushion in a glass case, and sent to the museum, where it is still on display to this very day!

The End